The
Name Soup

This book belongs to

. . . .

The Name Soup

by Sandhya Sameera
Pillalamarri

illustrated by Red Hansen

LION HEART
BOOKS

All of the educational pieces, etymology and historical references in this book are real.
The author has tried to maintain factual accuracy as best as possible. However, this is a
work of fiction. Names, characters, places, events, and incidents either are the
product of the author's imagination or are used fictitiously. Any resemblance to
actual persons, living or dead, events, or locales is entirely coincidental.

Illustrations copyright © 2014 by Red Hansen.
Design by Judy Linard.
Typeset in Candida and Hoagle.
The illustrations in this book were rendered digitally.

This book has been printed on 100% acid-free paper.
Digital links included may be outdated in the future given the changing
nature of the Internet.

The Library of Congress Cataloging-in-Publication Data
Pillalamarri, Sandhya Sameera.
The name soup / Sandhya Sameera Pillalamarri. First Edition.
p. cm.
Summary: Second-grader Leela hates her long and difficult last name. Through a series
of adventures she learns the meaning behind names and grows to love her own.
ISNB: 978-0-9907245-3-7 (hardcopy)
ISBN: 978-0-9907245-9-9 (trade)
[1. Names, Personal—Fiction. 2. Identity—Fiction. 3. Schools—Fiction.
4. Culture, Diversity—Fiction. 5. Asian Americans—Fiction.] I. Title.
2014914936

Printed in the United States of America

Published by Lion Heart Books LC
Boston, MA

www.thenamesoup.com

For my parents Indira and Sesh —
who taught me to dream big

For my husband Sarath —
who gave the freedom to chase my dream

And for my son Srikanth —
who became my ultimate dream come true

Contents

First Day of School

Leela Kongkitisoupchai had a long and unusual last name. And she hated it.

Well, at first, eight-year-old Leela couldn't have been happier. After all, today was the first day of school! She was super excited. So excited that she woke up bright and early to get ready and catch the school bus on time.

Leela lived in Sedona, Arizona – a beautiful state on the western side of America. Sedona has lots of thorny cactus plants, smooth red mountains

and long sunny days. And today was no exception. It was the perfect day to start second grade for the first time. Leela couldn't *wait* to meet all her old friends and make some new ones too. Leela liked her town and most of all she loved her friends.

Leela's *best* friends were Aleph Boker, Uma Rama and Tata Iyotake. When she got to school that day, she was thrilled to see that Uma was sitting right next to her desk in class. So awesome!

Leela's teacher, Mrs. Adams, was happy to see everyone at *Oak Creek Elementary* after the long summer break.

"Let's first begin with roll call to see who's in class, shall we?" Mrs. Adams adjusted her glasses and looked down at her binder.

"Amanda Chase?"

"Here!"

"Uma Rama?"

"Here!"

And this is when it all started going downhill.

Mrs. Adams came across Leela's name. Uh-oh! She paused, made a scrunching face as if in pain, took a deep breath and stumbled all over her last name.

"Leela Konga — tiki — no wait. Kong — ki — ti — soup — chai?!" Mrs. Adams looked *exhausted*.

Oh, no, no, **No**! She's got it completely wrong!

Well, Leela wasn't *that* surprised that Mrs. Adams couldn't say her name. This was not the first time that someone struggled with it. Many times she had heard her mom spell her last name over and over again at the doctor's office or on the phone with the airlines.

"K for Kite, O for Orange, N for Nancy . . . it is Kongkitisoupchai!" her mother used to say on the phone with an exasperated look on her face.

So Leela thought it best to let Mrs. Adams know how exactly to say her name too.

"Mrs. Adams, my name is Leela Kong-kiti-soup-chai!" she said slowly, opening her mouth wide and pausing at strategic breaks.

Amanda Chase ✓
Uma Rama ✓
Leela Kongtikisoupchai ☐
James Johnson ☐
Joyce Sweeney ☐

"Ah, thank you dear. I think I'll — er, um — just stick with Leela instead — much easier! Now where was I — ah yes — Liam Nelson?"

James thought that her name was pretty funny. Leela knew James W Johnson from her previous years in kindergarten and first grade. They never really got along. Well, *nobody* gets along with James except for Joyce Sweeney who follows James around like some kind of a puppet. Joyce thinks that this will make her popular in school. James was the kind of boy who looked down on other kids with his nose up in the air – like he was better than everybody else. He was also over a foot taller than Leela, which didn't help much.

"Hey Leela, I'm really hungry. Could you get me some soup and maybe some chai tea too while you're at it, please*ee*?" He acted clutching his stomach in mock hunger.

Why would I have soup or chai tea with me, though a confused Leela. James continued to give her a hard time. "You know, 'cause you are a something, something *Soup Chai* right? Hahahaha!" He sneered as he flicked a wad of paper onto Leela's desk.

Joyce overheard his comment and started to shiver and shake with laughter. Pretty soon the other kids in class joined in on the fun.

"Soup Chai, Soup Chai! Give us some soup and chai!" cried a few kids in chorus.

"Quiet out there!" yelled Mrs. Adams peering through her glasses as she searched for the perpetrators.

Leela felt very, *very* upset. Humph! This had never happened before. I guess this was the first time Mrs. Adams did roll call. But is everyone laughing at me because of my last name? Is my last name really *so* unusual and hard to say, she wondered.

Feeling Low

That whole day Leela could think of nothing else but her last name. She was puzzled – was she really named after a soup and chai tea? But how could that be? *That's* when she decided she didn't like her name very much. It was too long, hard to say, and just plain *weird*!

After school, she came home and sat sulking at the kitchen table. Leela wasn't the sulking type. But then again, she had never been made fun of before. Leela's grandmother was visiting Leela and her

family all the way from a small town in Thailand called Chai Nat. Grandma always wore a long skirt and a long top with her hair in a bun on top of her head. She too had freckles on her cheeks just like Leela did.

Grandma saw how upset Leela looked. "Why do you look so sad Leela? Is something wrong?" she asked with concern.

But Leela decided not to tell her . . . grandma wouldn't understand. Actually, she didn't feel like talking about it with *any*one! It was too embarrassing. Her cheeks burned as red as the smooth red rock canyons of Sedona when she recalled what had happened to her in class today. She turned her face away in a huff and continued to mope.

Just then, Leela's mom came home from work. She put her bag and keys down and came over to give Leela a soft kiss on the forehead. Mom was a chef at a popular Thai restaurant in town. Because of this, she had a chef's hat on most of the time, even when inside the house. Mom also always smelled of curry and fragrant jasmine rice. Normally, Leela would feel very happy to see her mother's gentle face. But not today. Today she was preoccupied.

"I have to go get groceries for tomorrow's event. Do you want to come with me?" mom asked, smiling. Oh, Leela had almost forgotten! Tomorrow night was the big talent show program at school and mom was in charge of catering the food for the event.

"Don't forget to prepare for the talent show tomorrow, children! It will be a gala night for our school and *everybody* will be there!" Mrs. Adams had reminded them in class. Most students had fair warning of the popular event because teachers pretty much talked about it all the way from kindergarten through first grade.

"I want each and every one of you to think of a special talent that you can showcase on stage . . . some of you might juggle balls, some might sing, and some might dance. Anything goes!" Mrs. Adams had said excitedly.

The talent show was the *last* thing on Leela's mind. There was no way she would go up on stage in front of everyone just so she could be made fun of again. Right now all Leela wanted to do was forget about her *annoying* last name which sounded like soup and chai.

Maybe she would go to the grocery store with mom. She did love all those bright lights, foods, and smells. The store even had free samples at times!

The talent show could wait.

A Trip to the Grocery Store

Sedona *Kosher Market* had the best organic produce and desserts in town. Leela's mom loved to shop there for special occasions. When they got to the store, Mrs. Kongkitisoupchai wanted to buy some banana bread from the bakery. As Leela stared at the mouth-watering chocolates and pastries behind the glass case, she suddenly spotted someone familiar. She was surprised to see her friend Aleph Boker sitting behind the baker's counter! Leela had known Aleph since first grade. Mr. Boker was there too. He was a tall and lanky man who never seemed to look up much. I guess he didn't have to. He was busy kneading dough on the counter top.

"Hey Aleph! What are *you* doing here?" Leela asked, peering through the glass case.

"Hiii Leela! I am helping my dad. This is our bakery shop!" Aleph stood up, wiping crumbs off his face. He was eating an apple strudel.

Leela didn't know that Aleph and his family owned a bakery shop.

"Do you want some?" asked Aleph offering his strudel to Leela. "No thanks" said Leela hesitantly, still surprised to see him here.

"I am sorry James made fun of you in class *foo . . .* day," he continued, talking with this mouth full of pastry.

Why did he have to remind her of James again, groaned Leela! She had come to the store to try and forget about him and her long last name.

"Hey, did you know that my last name is sort of funny too? It is Boker which actually means Baker in Hebrew!" he said with a grin. He started to dust off some of the powdered sugar that had fallen on his shirt.

Leela looked at him disbelievingly. He sure didn't look like a baker. And what's 'Hebrew' anyway, she thought.

Aleph's dad must have noticed the frown on Leela's face because he suddenly looked up from behind the counter and began to clarify. "Leela, did you know that Hebrew is a type of a language? Our family practices the Jewish religion and our last name is unique to our culture. Since my family has been in the baking business for a long, long time . . . well, we came to be known as the bakers -- or Boker in Hebrew!"

Wow. So last names can actually mean something – like a baker?

Come to think of it, Aleph did always bring the best desserts in his school lunch box.

Leela thought this was really interesting. Aleph's last name meant something. It meant that his family was full of bakers. His last name was so cool!

"Let's get going dear. I still need to buy some eggplant and wonton wrappers," said Mrs. Kongkitisoupchai hurriedly.

Leela hung her head a little low as they drove away from the store after finishing grocery shopping. Leela felt dejected. I bet my last name means nothing cool except for some yucky old soup and some stale cold chai tea, she declared to herself. She couldn't help but feel that Aleph's last name was so much more interesting than hers. Why can't my name be 'Boker' too? My last name is so long, uninteresting and *weird*, Leela thought.

Piano Class

After grocery shopping, Leela's mom dropped her off at piano class. Leela had piano classes every Monday evening at Uma's house. Uma's mom, Mrs. Rama, was once an accomplished pianist who now taught classes for young kids in her free time.

As Leela entered the house, she took a whiff of the spicy aromas coming from the kitchen.

"What's your mom cooking?" Leela asked Uma who ran up to say hello. Leela's stomach growled – she hadn't eaten anything after school.

"Hi Leela! Oh, that's mom's delicious samosas. She makes them for special occasions – especially for Diwali!" said Uma cheerfully.

What's 'Diwali' Leela thought. Just then, Mrs. Rama came out of the kitchen holding a platter full of little candle tea lights. In the darkened living room, the lights cast a golden shadow, flickering softly on her face.

"Diwali is the festival of lights in India, Leela" explained Mrs. Rama as she walked in. "Today is Diwali! We adorn our homes with little lamps called *diyas* to indicate the triumphant return of Lord Rama and Goddess Sita from their long exile in the jungle," said Mrs. Rama as she arranged the little lights in a neat row on the fireplace mantel.

Right above the mantel was a large portrait. Leela had never noticed it before until now.

"Who's in that painting Mrs. Rama?" inquired Leela.

Piano Class

"That's Lord Rama and Goddess Sita," she said, looking up.

"This painting depicts the day they got married. You see, Rama was the king's first born son. And Rama's step mother didn't like Rama very much and wanted her own son to become the king instead. So she devised an evil plan to send Rama and his wife Sita away to live in exile in the nearby forest for fourteen years," said Mrs. Rama.

Leela's eyes grew wide. That's awful! Leela felt sad for Lord Rama and his wife.

"Finally, after all those years in the jungle, Rama, Sita and even his step brother, who refused the king's crown and joined them in the jungle, all came back to the kingdom," Mrs. Rama continued.

That was very nice of his brother, thought Leela. I don't have a bother, but if I had to go into the jungle all by myself, I would want my brother to come along to keep me company too, imagined Leela.

"Everyone in the kingdom was so happy to see them again that they welcomed them with lots of good food. They even had fireworks. People celebrated their victorious return by adorning their homes with lots and lots of lights!"

Leela was fascinated. She thought it was really nice of the people to do that. She wouldn't want to live in a jungle even for *one* night, let alone fourteen long years! What if a tiger or a bear were to eat you? She let out a shiver at the thought of it.

Mrs. Rama went into the kitchen and brought out the plate of samosas. "I heard about how kids made fun of you in class today Leela. Uma told me. I'm very sorry to hear that. Kids can be very mean sometimes," said Mrs. Rama sadly.

Just as she was *trying* to forget about everything

that had happened today, Mrs. Rama had reminded her again. Leela groaned.

"Did you know, Leela, that our family's ancestors used to be high priests who prayed to Lord Rama and Goddess Sita? For generations together they used to take care of some of India's most famous temples. Kings and queens used to ask my great, great, great grandfather to help them celebrate Diwali in their kingdoms and palaces. That's how we came to be known as the 'Rama' family. That's why our last name is Rama," Mrs. Rama said.

Wow. So Uma's last name meant a great God and Goddess, thought Leela. Come to think of it, Uma often did have a wise, priestly look about her. Especially with all her straight-A grades in class. Uma's last name is so cool!

"Well, what are we waiting for? Let's hurry up and play the lessons on the piano so we can eat!" she Uma impatiently, eying the platter of warm samosas on the table.

But Leela didn't feel like playing on the piano anymore. She kind of felt jealous of Uma's name instead.

Leela was really quiet on the drive back home after piano class. Why can't my name be 'Rama' too, Leela thought grudgingly. My last name is definitely not as great as Uma's. It is just long and *boring*.

Feathered Hat

After getting home, Leela planned to grab a quick bite and hide out in her room upstairs. She wasn't feeling very happy.

But when they pulled into the driveway of their house, Leela did a double take. Her next door neighbor and *best* friend Tata was out on his driveway too. But Leela almost didn't recognize him. He was dressed in an elaborate costume!

She ran up to Tata to get a closer look. He was so proud of his new outfit. Tata strutted in front of Leela with his hands on his sides and his nose up in the air.

"Hey, how do I look?" he demanded.

Leela didn't know what to say . . . Tata was wearing a poncho-type jacket that had a blue turquoise stone dangling from its zipper, a pair of black leggings and a large feathered hat! He looked like someone really important.

Just then, Tata's mom, Mrs. Iyotake, walked out of the house.

"Leela, would you like to try on Tata's feathered headdress?" she offered politely.

Mrs. Iyotake was a short, cheerful woman who always had a smile on her face. "Go on Tata. Let her try it on for some time," she said. Tata did not want to remove his awesome hat. But he reluctantly gave it to Leela and let her put it on anyway.

Leela felt regal with the feathered hat on her head. She turned to look at herself in the reflection on Tata's car window.

"Today my friend is having a potlatch, or a gift-giving feast, to celebrate the birth of her new baby. Tata and I were invited and we thought it would be great for him to dress up like the powerful chief, Sitting Bull!" Mrs. Iyotake said, giving Tata a slight slap on his back. Leela was really intrigued. Who was 'Sitting Bull' and why was he named after a bull?

Tata's mom continued with a far-away look in her eyes. "You see, Leela, Sitting Bull was an important chief from the Hunkpapa Lakota tribe whose headdress was a warbonnet. Our family is of Native American origin and a long, long time ago we belonged to a Lakota tribe from the state of Dakota. We came to adopt the famous chief Tatanka Iyotake's name, which in the Sioux language actually means 'Sitting Bull'. Your friend Tata here is named after this chief in his honor!"

Wow. Come to think of it, Tata did always have the bravery of a mighty warrior. Leela thought that this was really amazing. Tata is named after a famous Native American chief. His name is so cool!

Mrs. Iyotake seemed to remember something just then. "I heard about some kids making fun of you in class Leela. Tata told me about it. Nobody should be made fun of for whatever reason. I am sorry it happened to you," she said with sympathy.

Ugh. Does the whole *world* have to know about this, thought Leela, exasperated.

She very much felt like disappearing away right then.

Glancing over at Leela's forlorn face, Tata's mom had an idea to try and make her happy. "Why don't you come with us to the party, Leela!" said Mrs. Iyotake. Anywhere else would be *much* better than here, thought Leela. Besides, she really did want to see what a potlatch was all about.

"Thanks Mrs. Iyotake. I would love to go if that's alright," said Leela. She ran over to her house to ask her mother if she could go. "Okk . . . but you have to be back before 8 o'clock. You need to come up with something to perform for the talent show.

And you promised to help me with the cooking," reminded mom.

"Oh I promise mom, thank you!" cried Leela as she raced to her room. She was excited again! She grabbed her backpack and hurried on over to Tata's.

As they drove off to the gift-giving feast, Leela was filled with curiosity. What would she see? Would other people dress up like the famous chief Tatanka Iyotake? I wish my name was 'Iyotake' too like the great chief, Leela yearned.

A Grand Party

When Leela got to the potlatch it was unlike anything she had ever seen. It wasn't just any old small party; it looked like a huge ceremony of some sort! There were lots of people walking around – some dressed up in Native American tribal clothing, just like Tata. Everyone seemed to be busy dancing, singing or talking, all at once. And there was a *lot* of food.

Leela was mesmerized with the bounty of food that was being served. There was roast corn, turkey, cranberries, beans, chili stew, and lots and lots of bread!

Seeing that they had arrived, the hosts of the potlatch came over to greet Mrs. Iyotake and Tata. They had a cute little baby in their arms. She was wrapped up in a cozy blanket. When they saw that Tata had brought along his friend, they bent down and gave Leela a warm hug and welcomed her to the celebration.

"Welcome to the birthing and naming ceremony of our little daughter Raven," they said. Their faces beamed with happiness.

They even had naming ceremonies?! Leela was astonished.

"What's Raven's last name?" she asked shyly.

"Oh our family doesn't really have a last name dear," said Raven's mother.

Can you *do* that? No last name? That sounded good to Leela. Maybe she'd get rid of her last name too!

The kind lady continued. "You see, long ago most Native Americans never had a family name. But when America was colonized by the English, we had to choose and create last names for us too. Now everyone has a family name and ours is Purser."

Oh *great*. So they did have a last name then, thought Leela, disheartened.

The couple with the baby asked Mrs. Iyotake to take a seat and walked away to greet other guests.

"Come on! Let's go eat," exclaimed Tata, grabbing Leela's arm. They sat at the round communal table, and Leela was served a lavish feast. She was very hungry by now. No matter how much she ate, her plate kept getting refilled with more food. In fact, Leela stuffed herself silly. Everything tasted *so* delicious! Her favorite dish was the fry bread. She learned that the fry bread was a traditional Native American bread served at most gatherings like a potlatch.

Just then the hosts of the party called everybody's attention. "Let's raise our glasses and make a toast to our new daughter Raven Purser!" announced the new parents proudly.

"We chose to name our daughter Raven after the Native American Raven God. Our daughter's birth symbolizes the positive change and magical transformation about to happen in our family with her birth. She will bring harmony to us," said the parents affectionately.

Leela watched in awe as all the adults shouted out their congratulations and raised their arms up in the air – clinking their glasses full of Hopi tea together, laughing boisterously.

Just after dinner was over, Mrs. Iyotake asked if Leela wanted to join Tata and all the little kids in a dance that was about to start. "This dance is called a cycle song-dance in our culture. We dance to honor the spirit of the Native American potlatch. I bet you can dance really well Leela," encouraged Mrs. Iyotake.

What's a 'cycle song-dance' wondered Leela. But before she could ask her what it meant, the dancing began! Someone started to sing a song and beat a set of drums rhythmically.

"See how the song is being sung in beats of nine Leela? Count out the beats and you'll hear it. This honors each of our guardian spirits and helps us receive their blessings for long lasting peace and prosperity," said Mrs. Iyotake.

Leela nodded her head in agreement. She didn't really understand everything Mrs. Iyotake said but she was amazed to learn that dancing could have so much meaning behind it too. *Every*thing here seemed to mean something.

She watched as Tata moved his arms and legs

in circles to the beat of the drums. She listened to the song and began to hum along with the beautiful music. Her feet automatically began to tap along as if wanting to dance. Leela felt transported to an ancient world where people always seemed happy. In this world no one would ever laugh at someone just because their last name was long and didn't mean anything interesting.

Presents

Eventually, it was time to leave the potlatch. Leela noticed that Raven's parents were giving something away to all the kids and the guests who had come to the ceremony. Leela also got a bag when she left!

On the drive back home, she opened it to find a ceramic carving in the shape of a horse that had no eyes, ears or mouth. Also in the bag was a strange looking wooden circle with a web in the middle and some feathers and beads hanging below it. Leela's mind raced with questions as she turned the objects over in her hands.

When Tata's mom pulled into their driveway, Leela showed her the horse and the web from the bag. "What are these Mrs. Iyotake?" she inquired.

"Oh, traditionally potlatches were a big deal. Some people spent a year planning for it! And each person who is invited to a potlatch receives a special present. The present is a gesture of love and thanks. In the olden days, presents used to be elaborate and a way for the hosts to show off their wealth and importance."

"Hey, I got the same presents too." Tata looked disappointed as he peered into his bag.

"That's right Tata. Everybody who attends a potlatch receives the same presents. This is one way for the hosts to treat everyone fairly," said Mrs. Iyotake, ruffling the feathers on Tata's head.

As Leela got out of the car to go home, Mrs. Iyotake called out to her. "Keep your presents somewhere safe Leela. We believe that the ceramic horse brings good luck to its owner. And the object with the feathers you have there is called a dream catcher. Some Native American tribes believe that as you sleep, the web in the middle traps all your bad dreams and lets only the good ones slip into your mind."

Leela was intrigued as she looked at her gifts. She turned over the horse and saw that it was marked on the back with the letters 'MPL'. Before she could ask more about the dream catcher or the horse, she saw her mom peering out their living room window.

"Leela, is that you? Could you please wash up and come help me with the cooking for tomorrow's show?" Leela waved to her mom and let out a sigh as she remembered the talent show.

She would have to think of *some* talent to showcase . . . if only she could avoid everyone hearing her last name when she was called up on stage.

"Goodnight Mrs. Iyotake. Thank you for taking me with you to the party. It was a lot of fun!" said Leela.

"And Tata . . . I think your last name is really cool, and I like your feathered hat," she said with a smile. Tata took a deep bow. So deep that he tumbled and made his hat fall off. Leela laughed at her silly friend as she turned to go.

"Goodnight dear. Sweet dreams to you!" Mrs. Iyotake whispered, softly – almost knowingly – as Leela ran home.

Dream Catcher

The sweet and comforting smell of fresh dumplings wafted in as Leela opened her front door.

"Did you have fun tonight?" asked Mrs. Kongkitisoupchai as she walked in.

Leela helped mom pack the dumplings she had made for the show. One, two, three . . . Leela counted a hundred of them as she dropped each dumpling into some warm curry broth her mom had set aside. Mom's cooking always did taste so good and comforting. But tonight Leela was too full from the potlatch. She told her mother all about it and showed her the presents she had gotten.

"We'll have to send them a thank you note . . . that was very kind of them to give you something too Leela," said mom, wiping her hands on her apron.

Leela was curious about the gifts in her bag. Why is the horse considered lucky to its owner? Did the dream catcher really work?

That night, after helping mom, Leela opened her tablet computer to search more about the horse. She did not find anything about the letters 'MPL' but she did learn that they might be an artist's initials – kind of like an exclusive signature. I wonder which famous Native American artist made this horse, Leela thought. It was a mystery she would solve later because suddenly she felt very tired. Leela started to yawn – she had had a long day! As soon as she laid her head on her soft pillow, Leela was sound asleep.

That night she dreamed of fry bread, the jungle, and feathers.

She also had another strange dream. In this dream she was all alone on an island and a huge *name* was chasing her. It was her name! It looked like her last name was out to get her with its long set of letters trying to grab at Leela.

She began to run. Leela saw a boat waiting in the ocean waters surrounding the island. The only way Leela could escape from the hideous chasing name was to get into the boat and row really fast to another island she could spot on the vast ocean.

When she got to this new island, she tried to rest on the shores of its beautiful beach. But her last name had other plans. It had gotten into another boat and chased her to the new island too! Leela then saw a big tree on the beach shore and climbed up one of its long trunks. She was safe up here . . . for now. But Leela seemed to know that it was only inevitable that she come face to face with the

Kongkitisoupchai

name waiting patiently for her at the base of the tree trunk.

Leela tossed and turned uneasily for the rest of the night.

She woke up early the next morning with a start. She saw that her mother had hung the dream catcher above her bed and put the horse on her writing desk. She wondered why the dream catcher had not trapped her strange dream last night. Maybe it didn't work?

As Leela brushed her teeth and got ready for school, she tried to recall the details from the dream. She had been on a boat and climbed some tree. But why? She couldn't really remember the entire dream.

"Breakfast is ready! Come down soon Leela or you'll miss your bus," yelled mom.

Oh well. This is just my imagination, thought Leela, dismissing the strange dream as she put on her clothes and hurried downstairs.

She was lost in thought as she stirred her spoon around in the cereal. Grandma seemed to notice that Leela was distracted. "Leela, you know you can talk to me about anything that's bothering you. Perhaps I can help," offered grandma.

Leela wanted to tell her *every*thing! About how everyone's names were awesome and meant something important. About how her name wasn't so cool and interesting at all. About how she didn't feel like going to school that day as it would mean she would have to face mean-faced James again.

But . . . grandmother wouldn't understand. After all, she was from Thailand and what would she know about her boring last name that no one could say. She would probably sip on some hot soup and tea, wrinkle her nose and think Leela was whining instead.

When Leela got to school that day, she tried to avoid running into James. There were still twenty minutes left before class started. She decided she could hide out in the school library until then. James never set foot in the library. He called it the 'geek' corner.

When she got to the library, Leela remembered the book on family trees – her teacher had mentioned it during class project last year. You see, last year everyone had to bring in pictures of their families to class to build a family tree. Perhaps there was something in there that could explain why her last name was so long and *weird*?

The librarian pointed Leela to the book and left her to it. She eagerly flipped through the pages but did not find anything related to her name. As she put the book down in frustration, another thick book lying on the same table caught Leela's eye.

There was a black and white photo of an older man on the front cover and some kind of a caption written underneath it. Even while the school bell rang signifying the start of class, Leela couldn't move. She was frozen. What she saw on the book cover stopped her cold in her tracks!

The Banyan Tree

Ten minutes later, Leela eventually got to her class looking gloomy. Mrs. Adams was very surprised at her tardiness since she was never late for school.

"I'll let it slide this time, Leela. Go find your seat," she said, with a firm voice.

But Leela scarcely heard what Mrs. Adams had said. She was lost in thought. The book she had been reading at the library had a caption underneath the black and white photograph of a rather important looking man. He had curly black hair and a stern look on his face. The caption had read 'James Weldon Johnson, The Great Civil Rights Activist'. Was mean-faced James named after this famous person too? Am I the *only* one in class who isn't named after somebody important or something interesting? She continued to dwell on it anxiously as Mrs. Adams began to teach the class about pronouns, adjectives and verbs.

The day seemed to drag on and on, class after class. Finally school was over and it was time to go home.

"Remember children . . . tonight is talent show night! I hope all of you have prepared something special to share on stage. See you in a few hours!" cried Mrs. Adams, clasping her hands with excitement.

Leela was anything *but* excited. She was really worried now. It was 2:30 in the afternoon and she still did not know what she was going to perform! Plus, she was sure everybody would laugh at her again when Mrs. Adams called her on the stage with her *troublesome* long last name.

After school, Leela came home more upset than ever before. She found her grandmother sitting at the kitchen table. Grandma motioned for her to come over.

"Tell me what's bothering you?" requested grandma once again, patiently.

This time, Leela couldn't stop herself. She ran over to her and told her *everything*.

"Grandma, why can't our last name be cool like everybody else's? Why does it have to be long and boring and so hard to say? I just *hate* it!"

"Well! Is that what's been upsetting my little Leela? Come, sit on my lap, and I will tell you all about it." Leela sat on grandmother's lap and buried her face into her shoulder, sobbing softly.

"There, there my child . . ." consoled grandma, stroking Leela's beautiful long black hair.

"Our name is hard to say because it is an absolutely

unique name. It means the wise old Banyan tree."
Leela's ears prickled and she sat up straight.

A tree?! She had dreamed of climbing a tree just
last night! But . . . trees aren't so cool.

"Our name means some boring tree, grandma?
Now everyone's going to make fun of me even *more* if
they ever find out," wailed Leela.

"It's not just any old tree Leela. There is a reason
behind it. Our last name came to us because a long,
long time ago our family used to live in China. *Kong* is a
popular Chinese last name. *Kong* is also the last name
of the great philosopher Confucius," grandmother
said thoughtfully.

But aren't we from Thailand, Leela puzzled
curiously.

"When war broke out, our family had to flee
from China in a hurry. So we got in a boat and came
to Thailand for safety. I was just a baby when this
happened. When we got to Thailand, the Thai officials
were very kind to us. They asked us to choose a last

name that also had a Thai meaning to it so we could blend into their culture better," continued grandma.

In my dream, there was a boat and I rowed very fast to another island, thought Leela excitedly.

"We settled in a small town in Thailand where there were *lots* of these Banyan trees. I used to play under its shady branches while I was growing up," said grandma smiling with a nostalgic look in her eyes.

"You see, the Banyan tree drops new roots from its branches every time it wants to grow! This makes the tree spread wide and live a long life. It is as if every few years new trees grow from the same old tree. And at the same time they are all connected to the main tree trunk. It is like a web of trees all inter-connected. They never separate from their main root. The banyan tree's aerial roots make it very strong and very mighty! Isn't that very clever of the tree?" said grandma, her eyes shining.

Leela indeed found the tree to be brilliant.

"The Banyan tree also gives lots of shade in the hot Thai summers to anyone who wants to sit under its big branches. It is said that the great Buddha Himself had sat under the Banyan tree to meditate," said grandma with reverence.

Leela knew who Buddha was – she saw his statue in her house every day! Leela's family is Buddhist.

"So, our family decided to change our last name to the Thai name *Kongkitisoupchai* as a way to represent our journey and the start of a new life in Thailand. '*Kong*' to represent our main roots to Confucius and China. '*Kitisoupchai*', which means 'of a good heart' in the Thai language, to represent the Banyan tree's kind-hearted nature, its unity and its strength!" said grandma proudly.

Leela couldn't contain her excitement anymore. Confucius was the greatest philosophers in the history of the world, her dad always said! Leela's dad often talked about Confucius at the dinner table, though Leela never understood most of what he said. Also, most trees don't have roots in the air – their roots are underground. This was a unique tree! And it was also a *kind* tree. It was a *clever* tree.

Wow! She jumped up from grandma's lap and hopped into the air.

"Yipeeee! My last name is so, *so* cool! It does not mean soup or chai tea. It isn't weird at all!" she rejoiced.

She was so proud of her last name now. Leela swelled up with joy thinking about what it meant and the story behind her name. She gave grandma a huge hug and ran up to her room. The dream catcher did work after all, she thought with wonder. It sent her the best dream she had ever had.

Suddenly, Leela knew exactly what she was going to do that night for the talent show. She couldn't wait!

Talent Show

"Leela Konga — tiki — no, no. Let's see now, *um*, Kong — ki — ti — soupchai?!" Mrs. Adams called shakily.

Several kids stared to chuckle as Leela stood up from her cozy seat in the audience. The talent show was underway. Some kids had juggled balls, some had sung songs, and some had even danced – just like Mrs. Adams had predicted. Leela had sat nervously waiting for her name to be called.

Then it was time for her to show her talent.

Leela slowly climbed the stairs up to the stage and cleared her throat when she took the microphone from Mrs. Adams.

Everyone fell silent.

"Ever since I could remember, people had trouble saying my last name. Well, I guess it is kind of long, and I guess it does sound *kinda* funny in English with the words 'soup' and 'chai' in it. But I never noticed it until yesterday when Mrs. Adams did roll call in our class for the first time."

Mrs. Adams turned bright red.

Leela continued without hesitation. She was starting to become brave. "At first I was really embarrassed about it. I hated it! How could my parents give me such a funny, long and *weird* name, I used to think. Then I had a lot of adventures yesterday that made me realize that everyone's names are different and unique. That names come from somewhere. Last names mean something! Sometimes they might even mean nothing. So, today for the talent show, I am going to give a speech on where last names come from and what they mean," declared Leela, confidently.

She could hear James grunting in the front row. She looked down just in time to see him roll his eyes. "Boring!" he yelled, loud enough for Leela to hear.

"Well, did you know, James, that your full name is actually James Weldon Johnson?" Leela said, looking at James. He looked positively shocked that Leela had the guts to speak to him directly!

"I spoke to your parents just before our show started. They told me that they named you after the great American author, lawyer, song writer, and civil rights activist by the same name."

James' jaw dropped. He hadn't expected to be put in the spot light!

"When I was in the library this morning, I saw a book about this famous man who fought for the rights of the African-American people. He was also the first African-American professor at New York University. His name was James Weldon Johnson. And your last name Johnson is one of the most common names in Europe and America and it means 'son of John' from Christianity – which is a religion by the way."

Leela looked quite scholarly as she peered at James from the stage. She was secretly thrilled to see that James seemed to have no idea about the meaning behind his name. He seemed to retreat further and further into his seat shyly.

"And where are you Joyce Sweeney? Oh there you are, right behind James on the second row," pointed Leela. There was a hushed sound as everyone turned to look at Joyce.

"Did you know that your name means 'Happy Dreamer'? Joyce in the Latin language actually means 'happy' and Sweeney means 'to dream'?"

Joyce, who was caught off-guard, spat out the gum she had been chewing for over ten hours. "Did she just talk about me?" Joyce asked incredulously to the boy sitting next to her.

Leela continued her speech explaining how her

day went by yesterday. She told everyone about the potlatch and the great Indian chief. She described to everybody the grand festival of lights called Diwali.

"Sometimes last names came from ancient times and sometimes they came from other people and things," she explained. She looked at her friends Aleph, Uma, and Tata fondly as she spoke of their names.

Little Leela commanded everyone's attention. She said that sometimes a last name meant a baker, a God, or even a kind and strong tree!

Leela spoke about the Banyan tree that her grandmother played under all those times back in Thailand. She told everyone how her family had fled from China and arrived in Thailand and settled near a town full of Banyan trees. She told them about the great Confucius and the wise Buddha.

Grandma, who was seated in the audience, listened to Leela with tears of joy in her eyes. Leela finally had her identity and felt proud of her last name!

When she finished talking there was a marked

silence in the auditorium. Then the crowd stood up with a thunderous roar of applause. Everyone cheered Leela as she walked off the stage.

Mrs. Adams gave her a big hug and thanked her for speaking about the importance of one's name. She agreed that nobody should feel ashamed of where they came from or how their name sounded.

Even James seemed to admire Leela's courage as he looked at her walking back to her seat, head held high.

That night, as Leela lay in bed, she looked at the ceramic horse on her desk and wondered if it had brought her the good luck she needed to do well in the talent show.

Did it help her look past her long last name and realize its true strength and beauty? She could never know.

But Leela was sure that her name was no longer long and weird. Instead, it was very interesting and very unique!

Leela feel asleep peacefully that night as a soft breeze floated in through her bedroom window, gently lifting and rattling the dream catcher above her bed.

Fun Exercises

(For use by readers, parents or teachers)

Our name makes us different from everyone else. It makes us unique. It identifies us. Sometimes it can trace us back to our ancestors and the struggles or successes they faced. Other times, it can even help us find meaning and a cause to our lives. In today's classrooms and neighborhoods, children come across many different ethnicities and names. They might be curious as to why someone's name is different, long or hard to pronounce.

Children, parents and teachers can use this section of the book and the following exercises as a way to help talk about diversity and inclusiveness. Children can use these exercises to cultivate their interview skills, form new friendships, and gain appreciation as to why their parents chose their unique name for them.

Use these exercises with your children / students to:

- *Interview* and *discuss* where people come from
- *Pronounce* difficult and long words/names
- Learn word *sounds* and *alliterations* found within names
- Research *origin* of names and their unique meanings.

Other possible ideas to explore are world festivals and events such as Diwali from India, Eid from Islamic countries, La Tomatina Festival from Spain, etc. (not included here).

These exercises can be a fun start to the year for 2nd

or 3rd graders or a way to end the year in Kindergarten. For older children, these can be the start of a program in social studies, literature, or geography to get children to think about world history, etymology, and genealogy in grades such as 4th, 5th or the 6th.

Parents and teachers will find the following exercises and worksheets here:

- Etymology Interview: What does my Name Mean?
- Pronunciation Guide (Computer Activity): Say My Name
- Genealogy Exercise (Computer Activity): My Family Tree

Interview: What Does My Name Mean?

My First Name: ....

My Middle Name: ....

My Last Name: ....

Interview Questions

(Interview your parents, grandparents, aunts
or uncles. Or, you can go to the Internet
URL: http://www.behindthename.com to find out more.)

What is your name?

Do you have a middle name?

What does your name mean?

What does my name mean? Why was I named (insert name)?

Am I named after someone or something?

Where are we from?

What is the meaning of our family name/last name?

Where did it come from?

What were your grandfather and grandmother's names?

Prounincation Guide: Say My Name

My First Name: ....

My Middle Name: ....

My Last Name: ....

Open your computer or other device such as a tablet and type
in the Internet URL: http://www.pronouncenames.com/

- In the 'Name' search box, type in your first name. Repeat this
  exercise for your middle and last name too.

- From the results page, write down the Pronunciation of
  your name: write out the letters as shown

- Now share it with your family, friends, or your class!

Genealogy Exercise: What Is My Family Tree?

Have you ever heard of the Census?

The United States government and most other governments around the world, keep a record of the number of births and deaths (among other information such as income) about every family in a town, state, and country. This record helps the government understand the amount of population in their country and plan for resources such as roads, hospitals, schools, houses etc.

Let's learn about your family history!

- Open your computer or tablet and type in the Internet URL: http:/www.ancestry.com

- Once there, click on the 'Get Started' button.

- Type in your name (first and last) and other required information.

- Find out what comes up and use the information to help you draw your family tree. Then share it with your family or your class!

(Then fill in the ovals on the family tree at the ends of this book!).

A Leela Kongkitisoupchai Adventure:

Book Two

by
Sandhya Sameera Pillalamarri

illustrated by Red Hansen

LION HEART
BOOKS

Going International

(Sneak Preview of Book Two)

"Leela, we are running late. Get in the car NOW!" hollered mom.

Leela Kongkitisoupchai was busy stuffing her last minute 'emergency' *stuff* into her suitcase; her hair brush, alarm clock, and pink Koala bear that she bought with her own pocket money last summer. After all, she would be gone for three whole weeks. There's no telling *what* she might need all the way over in Chai Nad, a small town half way across the world. Leela was about to leave for the airport to go on a long journey to Thailand over the winter break!

It was the start of the winter holidays in beautiful Sedona, Arizona where Leela lived and attended *Oak Creek Elementary*. Leela's best friends Aleph Boker, Uma Rama, and Tata Iyotake were all traveling to different places during the break too.

A week before school let out for the holidays, Aleph told everyone that he was taking a trip to Colorado to visit his aunt and uncle's 100 year old barn. They would be celebrating Hanukkah there. Aleph's family was Jewish.

"My uncle said that we would be going show shoeing this winter. Have any of you done it before?" he asked curiously. Neither of them had ever snow shoed before. So Aleph felt pretty proud of his winter plans. After all, he was going to be doing something interesting that his friends had never done before.

Then, a day later, Tata declared that he and his

family were going away to a native reservation in Tucson, Arizona. Tata was Native American. He talked about how he would be going fishing, swimming in the blue lake and camping by the bonfire.

And *then*, the next day, Uma announced that she and her family were going to Las Vegas to celebrate New Year's Eve in style. They were also going to attend a special concert by a famous Indian musician called A. R. Rahman. Uma's family was from India, and she knew all of A.R. Rahman's famous songs.

By now, Leela was starting to feel left out. Even though she was very happy for her friends, she was afraid that she would be stuck in Sedona all alone, all winter long. But the night before the last day of school, Leela's parents surprised her with tickets to Thailand!

Leela's family was going to drop her grandmother off back in her home town in Thailand called Chai Nad. Grandma had been visiting Leela's family at the start of the school year when Leela began second grade.

When Leela told Aleph, Uma and Tata of her winter plans the next day, they all agreed that Leela's trip was the coolest of them all. None of them were going on an international trip! Leela could barely contain her excitement. She was grinning from ear to ear. That's all she could talk about the entire day. About how she was going to visit her cousins, uncles and aunts and explore her home country.

Leela had never been to Thailand before. Mom told Leela that they were going to be visiting a big city called Bangkok, a remote jungle in Chiang Rai, and a beautiful beach in Koh Samui. Leela couldn't remember all the city names, but she was really excited to be going to a city, a jungle and a beach – all at once! Wow. This was going to be so much *fun*!

"Leela Phungusar Kongkitisoupchai!" screamed mom.

Leela winced. When mom referred to her by her *full* name, it meant serious business. She'd better hurry. Leela quickly grabbed her lucky horse and dream catcher from above her bed and rushed downstairs. She had received the horse and dream catcher at the beginning of the school year when she attended a special party for Native Americans called a potlatch. Ever since then, Leela never them out of her sight.

What will she see in Thailand? What will she eat? What secrets does Thailand hold for Leela? She couldn't wait to find out!

Acknowledgements

I am grateful to Amanda Hall for her guidance without which this book wouldn't have looked the way it does today. I wish to thank Melizza Santram-Chernov, an amazing illustrator, for her unvarying encouragement and for loving the concept of the book from day one.

Thanks to my wonderful editor Joyce Sweeney who is truly a happy dreamer. Many thanks to my astute designer Judy Linard for doing such a brilliant job with the book – and for all the pearls of wisdom along the way. I would also like to acknowledge Justin Rucker for connecting me with the very talented Red Hansen. And thank you Red for bringing Leela and her friends to life so beautifully.

Heartfelt gratitude to my sister and brother – Sirisha and Vamsee Pillalamarri – and to my friend, Usar Iamrod, for always being there. My eternal respect to my grandparents, the late Pillalamarri Uma Bala and Ramadas, the late Dantu Sita Rama Sastry garu and my grandmother Anasuya.

Much love to my extended Pillalamarri, Dantu, Akkineni and Nori family who continue to support me and whom I am proud to call my own.

About the Author

Sandhya Sameera Pillalamarri has always had a unique last name. And she is quite proud of it. When she isn't busy researching names, Sandhya can be found leading the research and evaluation strategy for a world premier educational technology and learning company. Sandhya has worked for multinational corporations in various leadership and consultative roles, driving product design & user experience for top digital and physical consumer products. She has studied computer science from Arizona

State University, human computer interaction from Carnegie Mellon University and management, strategy and operations from Harvard University. Sandhya can be found cooking, reading and pronouncing her toddler's Sanskrit name somewhere in the suburbs of Boston, MA. This is her first book.

CPSIA information can be obtained at www.ICGtesting.com
Printed in the USA
LVOW02s0826040315

429190LV00021B/94/P